THE EASY WAY

By Eleanor Robins

D0040466

Development: Kent Publishing Services, Inc.
Design and Production: Signature Design Group, Inc.
Illustrations: Jan Naimo Jones

SADDLEBACK PUBLISHING, INC.
Three Watson
Irvine, CA 92618-2767

E-Mail: info@sdlback.com
Website: www.sdlback.com

ISBN 1-56254-683-X

Printed in the United States of America

1 2 3 4 5 6 08 07 06 05 04 03

Chapter 1

Laine was at her locker. Tess was there too. Tess was her best friend. And they had the same locker.

Tess was waiting for Laine to get her history book. Then they were going to class. They were in the same history class. It was their last class of the day. Miss Brent was their teacher.

Laine saw Ben walk by. He was in her science class.

Laine said, "Ben is cute. I would like to date him. Do you think he might ask me for a date?"

Tess said, "Not any time soon. He just started dating someone new. But he might ask you later."

Laine was still looking at Ben.

Tess said, "Come on, Laine. We need to get to class. Miss Brent always starts class on time. And you know what she does to kids who are late."

Miss Brent made them stay after school for 30 minutes. And they had to work on their history.

Laine got her book. And the girls went to class.

They quickly went to their desks. They didn't get to sit near each other. Laine sat on one side the room. And Tess sat on the other.

The bell rang.

Miss Brent said, "Open your books."

Laine didn't want to open her book. But she did.

She liked Miss Brent OK. But she did not like history.

Laine looked over at the next row. She saw Griff. He was looking at her.

Laine tried to keep her mind on history. But she did not try very hard.

Laine looked at Griff five or six more times. And he was always looking at her. She wished he would stop looking at her.

Laine was glad to hear the bell. She liked school OK. But she was glad when school was over.

She wanted to go home and shoot some baskets.

Laine and Tess started to walk to their locker.

Laine said, "I don't have a lot of homework. How about you?"

"Just in math," Tess said.

Laine said, "Good. Come over to my house. We can shoot some baskets."

Tess said, "I can't right now. Maybe later. I am going to the track to run some. Do you want to run with me?"

Laine said, "Not me. I want to be on the basketball team. Not the track team. And it isn't fun just to run. Come home with me. And shoot baskets with me."

"I need to run," Tess said.

"Why?" Laine asked.

"To get in shape for basketball. Practice starts next week. Come to the track with me. We can run now. And shoot baskets later," Tess said.

"Running will not help me shoot baskets better," Laine said.

Tess said, "Sure it will. It will get you in better shape."

"You can get in better shape that way. I don't need to. You go on and run. I am going home," Laine said.

"At times I don't think you care about playing basketball," Tess said.

That surprised Laine. How could Tess say that?

Laine said, "Sure I do. I spend a lot of time shooting baskets at home. And that is why I am so good at it."

Laine had been the highest scorer on the team last year. Tess had been on the team too. But not on the starting team.

"There is more to playing basketball than shooting baskets," Tess said.

Laine laughed. She said, "Not when you shoot baskets as well as I do."

Chapter 2

It was the first day of basketball practice. Laine was in the gym. Tess was there too. Laine was ready to shoot baskets. But she knew she had to wait.

"I can hardly wait for the first game," Laine said.

Tess laughed. She said, "Not so fast, Laine. We have a lot of work to do before then."

"I don't want to think about that," Lainc said.

Laine did not like to practice. She just wanted to play in the games.

"Do you think we will both make the starting team?" Tess asked.

Laine looked to see who else was

there. She saw Val and Deb. They were in her history class. She knew most of the other girls too.

"I think we will," Laine said. She was sure she would.

Tess said, "I think you will too. And I think Deb will. But I am not sure about Val and me."

Coach Yates blew her whistle. Then she said, "We have a lot to do today. So we need to get started."

Laine was ready.

Coach Yates had a sheet of paper in her hand. She said, "You should have signed up last week. So all of your names should be on this list."

She called out the names. And all of the girls were on the list.

Coach Yates said, "All of you need to be able to shoot well. From the free throw line. And from all over the court.

You need to know how to dribble. How to pass. And how to guard the other team."

Laine said, "I wish Coach Yates would stop talking. And let us play."

But only Tess could hear what Laine said.

Coach Yates said, "You need to be in good shape to win. So you need to run some on your own."

Laine did not like to run. So she didn't plan to run on her own.

Coach Yates said, "Don't forget this. You need to have good teamwork. That is what makes a winning team. And I know all of you want to win."

All the girls yelled as loudly as they could.

Coach Yates said, "We will start all of our practices with running drills. Then do stretches."

Laine was ready to play. Not to do drills and exercises.

She did the drills and exercises. But she was tired after she did them.

Chapter 3

It was the next day. Laine was in history class. It was almost time for class to start. And Tess was not there.

Griff came in. He walked by Laine's desk. But he did not have to walk by Laine's desk.

Tess came in. She quickly went over to Laine. Tess looked worried. She had a history book in her hand.

Laine said, "What's wrong?"

"This is your book. My book wasn't in our locker. Do you have it?" Tess said.

Laine said, "I don't know. I didn't look. I just got a book."

Tess said, "Please don't take my book

again. I was worried because I couldn't find it. I knew I didn't leave it at home."

Laine didn't know why Tess was so upset. Tess had a book. So why did it matter that Laine got the wrong book? A book was a book.

Tess said, "I thought I had lost my book. And I thought I'd be late to class."

Tess quickly gave Laine the book she had. She got her book from Laine. Then she hurried to her desk.

The bell rang just as Tess sat down. She was almost late.

Miss Brent said, "Get out your homework. We will go over it. So you can check your answers."

Laine got her homework out.

Miss Brent said, "Tess, you tell us the first answer."

Laine looked at Griff. He was looking at her.

Tess read her answer.

Miss Brent said, "Very good, Tess. All of you be sure to know that."

But Laine didn't know what Tess had said. She was too busy looking at Griff to listen.

Miss Brent said, "Laine, you do the next one."

Laine quickly read her answer.

"That was OK, Laine. But you should have had more," Miss Brent said.

Laine did not care as long as her answer was OK.

The class went over the rest of the homework. Laine looked at Griff a few more times. He was looking at her. She wished he would stop looking at her.

The class read some pages in the book. Then the bell rang.

Laine got her books. She started for the door. Tess was walking with her. They were in a hurry to get to the gym. They didn't want to be late to basketball practice.

Griff bumped into Laine.

"Look where you are going, Griff," Laine said.

Griff didn't say anything. He just walked out the door.

Tess laughed. She said, "Griff was looking where he was going. He just bumped you so you would see him. And say something to him. I think he wants to date you."

Laine said, "He is OK. But I don't want to date him. And I wish he would stop looking at me in class."

"How do you know he does?" Tess asked.

"I look at him. And he is always looking at me," Laine said.

Tess laughed. She said, "Maybe you should stop looking at him. Then maybe he would stop looking at you. You two need to listen in class more. And look at each other less."

Chapter 4

Laine wanted to be on the basketball team. So she went to all of the practices. And she did the drills and exercises. But she did not want to do them.

Drills and exercises were not any fun. She just wanted to shoot baskets. And play in the games.

And she did not run on her own. But Tess did.

Laine could hardly wait for the first game. It would be with Glen High. And it would be a home game.

The days seemed to pass slowly for Laine. But then the big day came. The team would play Glen High after school.

Laine and Tess were on the starting team. And so was Deb. Val was one of the subs.

Laine saw Tess in the hall.

Tess said, "I can hardly wait. The game will start in only a few hours."

"I feel the same way," Laine said.

Tess said, "You can't be as excited as I am. You were on the starting team last year. But this will be my first time to start."

But Laine was very excited too. She hoped to be the high scorer again. And she could hardly wait to make a lot of baskets.

Tess said, "I still can't believe it. I wasn't sure I would make the starting team."

"You should have made it. You worked hard at practice," Laine said.

Laine did not work that hard. But it

didn't matter. She could score a lot of baskets. And no one else on the team could score that many. So she didn't have to work as hard.

The school day went by slowly for Laine. And she thought school would never end.

She was glad when the end of school bell rang.

Laine and Tess went quickly to the gym.

Tess said, "I hope I can play the whole game. And not get too tired. I want to play the best I can. And I can't do that when I am tired."

Laine wasn't worried she would get tired. All she cared about was scoring a lot of points.

Soon the game started. Carter High got the ball first. Tess passed the ball to Laine. Laine dribbled to the basket.

And then she scored two points.

"Way to go, Laine. Keep it up," one of the Carter girls said.

It wasn't long until Laine had scored six points. And it was Carter High 6 and Glen High 0.

Glen High called a timeout.

The Carter girls ran over to Coach Yates.

Laine said, "It will be easy for us to beat this team."

Coach Yates said, "It is too soon to know that. The game has just started."

"But they can't guard me well. So I will be able to score a lot of points. And it will be an easy win for us," Laine said.

Carter got a good lead. Then Glen High slowed the game down. So Carter could not score as many points.

Laine got tired. So she was glad Glen High slowed the game down.

Carter got far ahead. So Coach Yates put in subs. Laine was glad she did. It gave Laine some time to rest.

Laine had been right. It was an easy win for Carter High.

And Laine was the high scorer.

The next two games were easy wins for Carter High too. Carter got far ahead. The other teams slowed the games down. Coach Yates put in subs. So Laine got to rest when she got tired.

And Laine was the high scorer in those games too.

Chapter 5

Laine was in history class. Tess was there too.

The class had a test the next day. Miss Brent was telling the class what to study.

"You need to know the dates we talked about. And what the people did," Miss Brent said.

Laine knew most of that. She was sure she could get a C on the test.

Miss Brent was still talking. She said, "The test is hard. Be sure you study. So it won't be hard for you."

The bell rang.

Miss Brent said, "Stay after class, Laine. I want to talk to you."

"OK," Laine said.

She didn't know why Miss Brent wanted to see her. She hoped Miss Brent didn't talk to her for very long. She needed to get to basketball practice. And she could not be late.

Griff walked over to her desk. He said, "You must be failing this class."

"I am not. I am passing," Laine said.

Griff laughed. And then he started to the door.

Tess hurried over to Laine.

"What do you think Miss Brent wants?" Tess said.

"I don't know," Laine said.

"I thought you were passing," Tess said.

"I am. I have a C," Laine said.

"Hurry and find out what Miss Brent wants. I will wait for you in the hall," Tess said.

Tess hurried out of the classroom.

Laine got her books. She walked over to Miss Brent's desk. She said, "What do you want to see me about?"

"Your grade in this class," Miss Brent said.

"Why? I have a C," Laine said.

"But you could do so much better, Laine. Study a little more. And you could have a B. Maybe a low A," Miss Brent said.

Laine said, "Why? I can pass with a C."

"Don't you want to do the best you can?" Miss Brent asked.

Laine said, "Why? I don't need to do better. I am passing. So I don't need to study more."

"Don't try to take the easy way through school, Laine. Put out a little effort. And learn more," Miss Brent said.

Laine was learning as much as she wanted to learn. Why make it harder for herself? She liked the easy way.

"Don't study too little, Laine. And let your grade drop to an F," Miss Brent said.

"My grade won't drop to an F," Laine said.

"I hope it won't, Laine. But think about what I said," Miss Brent said.

"OK," Laine said. But she didn't plan to try to do any better.

Laine hurried out in the hall. Tess was waiting for her.

"What did Miss Brent want?" Tess asked.

"To talk to me about my grade. She thinks I should study more. And try to get an A or B," Laine said.

Tess said, "She is right. You should."

Laine was not surprised that Tess said that. Tess studied a lot. But Laine thought Tess tried too hard to do well.

Tess said, "Val is coming over to my house after practice. And so is Deb. We are going to study for the test."

"Why do you study with Deb? She can't read," Laine said.

Tess said, "Yes, she can. But just not very much. And she helps Val and me study. We read things to her. And she helps us to know what things mean. And how they fit together. Come over and study with us."

Laine said, "Thanks. But no. I don't like history. I can get a C on the test. So I am not going to study for it."

Tess said, "You should. Your grade isn't that good. You might get an F on the test. And that might pull you down to an F in the class."

"I won't get an F," Laine said.

Chapter 6

Laine and Tess went to their locker. Then they hurried to the gym.

Tess said, "I saw Griff say something to you. Did he ask you for a date?"

Laine said, "No. He thought I was failing the class. I told him I wasn't. He acted like he didn't believe me. And he laughed. Sometimes I think he tries to make me mad."

Tess said, "I told you before. I think Griff wants to date you. And that is why he acts that way."

Maybe Tess was right. Maybe Griff did want to date her.

Tess said, "Griff might ask you for a date. You said before that you didn't want to date him. Do you still feel that way? Or do you think you might like to date him?"

"I don't know. Maybe," Laine said.

Laine wasn't sure. She still wanted to date Ben. But she didn't think he would ask her. At least not any time soon. And it might be fun to date Griff.

Laine and Tess went in the gym. They put their books down. And they got ready to practice.

Laine got a ball. And she shot a few baskets before practice started.

Coach Yates blew her whistle.

Laine rolled the ball over to a corner.

"Time to run," Coach Yates said.

The team did some running drills. Laine saw Coach Yates looking at her.

Then the team did some stretching exercises.

"Now practice your passing," Coach Yates said.

"I will get a ball," Laine told Tess. She hurried to get one.

Laine and Tess threw the ball back and forth to each other. They passed to the left. And they passed to the right. They threw high passes. And they threw low passes.

Coach Yates walked over to Laine and Tess. She told Tess to practice passing with Val and Deb.

Tess walked over to Val and Deb.

Coach Yates looked at Laine. She said, "Have you been running some on your own?"

"Yes," Laine said.

Laine didn't want to lie to Coach Yates. But the coach had told them to run. And Laine wasn't going to say she had not been.

Coach Yates said, "I wasn't sure you had been. You seem to get tired before the other girls do. Are you feeling OK, Laine?"

She looked worried about Laine.

"I feel fine," Laine said.

Coach Yates said, "I am glad to hear that. So why don't you play better?"

That surprised Laine very much.

"I score more points than anyone else," Laine said.

Coach Yates said, "Yes, you do. But that is all you do well. You could be a very good basketball player. Maybe a great one. But you would have to put out more effort than you do now."

That surprised Laine even more. How could Coach Yates say that? Laine put out a lot of effort.

Chapter 7

Coach Yates went to help Val with her passing. Tess came back over to Laine.

Tess said, "You look upset. What did Coach Yates say?"

"She asked if I ran some on my own," Laine said.

"What did you tell her?" Tess asked.

"That I did," Laine said.

"How could you lie to her like that?" Tess asked. She looked upset with Laine.

Laine said, "So what? It doesn't matter. It was only a little lie. And I didn't want Coach Yates to get upset."

"But you should not have lied. What else did Coach Yates say?" Tess said.

"She asked how I was feeling," Laine said.

"Why did she ask you that?" Tess said.

"She thinks I get tired before the other girls do," Laine said.

Tess said, "You do. But that wouldn't have upset you. What else did she say?"

Laine didn't want to tell Tess. But she wanted to talk to someone about it. And Tess was her best friend. And Tess would know Coach Yates was wrong.

Laine said, "She said I need to play better. That I need to put out more effort."

"You do," Tess said.

That surprised Laine. How could her best friend say that?

"How can you say that?" Laine asked.

Tess said, "You work hard on what you like. But you don't work hard on what you don't like. You take the easy way on things you don't like."

"So? I am not the only person like that," Laine said.

Tess said, "I know. But you are the only one on the team like that."

"Maybe I am. But why should that matter?" Laine asked.

Tess said, "You are hurting the team. You play more for yourself than for the team."

That surprised Laine. How could Tess think that?

"How can you think that?" Laine asked.

Tess said, "You don't do your part. So the rest of us have to play harder."

Laine said, "I do my part. I score more points than anyone else does."

Tess said, "I know you do. But there is more to playing basketball than just scoring points."

Laine said, "Maybe so. But you have to score points to win."

Tess said, "But that won't win a game. You have to help to keep the other team from scoring too."

"I do that," Laine said.

Tess said, "But at times you get tired. And the team has to help you guard your player."

"That is not fair. We all have to help each other," Laine said.

"But we have to help you a lot," Tess said.

Chapter 8

It was Friday. Laine was in history class. Miss Brent had started class.

Miss Brent said, "I am going to give your tests back. A few of you did not do well. I told you the test would be hard. You should have studied."

Laine wasn't worried. She didn't study. But she knew she did OK. And she had told Tess she did. So Tess would know Laine did not need to study with her.

Miss Brent said, "You will have another test Monday."

Griff said, "Monday? You are going to give us a test on Monday?"

"Yes, Griff. That will give you all

weekend to study. And some of you need all weekend to study," Miss Brent said.

Then she told Griff to help pass out the tests.

Griff walked over to Deb's desk. He looked at her test. Then he handed it to her. She looked happy.

Griff passed out some more tests. Then he walked over to Laine's desk.

He looked at her grade. Then he said, "Too bad, Laine. You should have studied."

Griff laughed. Then he handed Laine her test.

Laine looked at her grade. An F! How could she get an F?

She quickly looked at her test. She had mixed up some of the people. And she had mixed up some of the dates. Why did they have to learn dates?

Now she had an F in the class. She should have studied with Tess. And with Val and Deb. But it was too late to think about what she should have done.

Laine could hardly wait for class to be over. She hurried out the door as soon as she could. She did not wait for Tess.

Laine was glad she had a game after school. She wanted to think about basketball. And not about her history test.

Tess called to her. She said, "Wait, Laine."

Laine stopped. And Tess hurried over to her.

Tess said, "Why are you in such a hurry? What did you make on the test?"

Laine didn't want to tell Tess her grade. But she did.

Tess looked surprised. She said, "You said you did OK on the test."

Laine said, "I thought I did. But the test was too hard."

Tess said, "Not for me. And not for Val and Deb. You should have studied with us. I asked you to."

Laine should have studied with them. But she wasn't going to tell Tess that.

Chapter 9

Laine and Tess hurried to the gym. The game was a home game. And they were going to play Hillman High. It was their first game with Hillman.

Most of the time Hillman had a good team. But this year they didn't. They had won only one game.

"We have had a great year so far. I hope we win this game too," Tess said.

Laine said, "Don't worry. We will. We have the better team."

Laine wasn't worried about the game. She was sure Carter High would win.

Tess said, "Hillman likes to run a lot. I hope they don't tire us out."

Laine wasn't worried about that. Carter High would get off to a quick lead. Then Hillman would slow the game down. So Carter would not score so many points.

Laine might get tired. But by then Carter would be far ahead. And Coach Yates would put in subs. And Laine would get to rest some.

It was time for the game to start. Laine was ready to play.

Laine looked at the girl who was going to guard her. The girl's name was Nan. Nan was not as tall as Laine. Maybe Laine could score her all time high in points.

The game started. Soon Laine scored.

Laine looked at Nan. She said, "That was only my first basket. I plan to make a lot more. Maybe even score my all time high in points."

Laine thought that would upset Nan. So Laine might be able to score more points. But Nan did not get upset.

"You might score a lot of points in other games. But not in this one," Nan said.

Laine said, "I will. I don't think you can guard me that well."

Nan said, "I don't have to guard you well. You won't be in the game that long. You aren't in good shape. Soon you will be too tired to play."

Laine said, "You're wrong. I'm in good shape. And I will score a lot of points."

But Laine knew she was not in good shape. She had to score a lot of points fast. Before she got tired.

Hillman kept the ball moving at a fast pace. Carter High tried to slow the game down. But Hillman did not let Carter do that.

Soon Laine was tired. She was still able to score points. But not as many as in some games.

"I knew you would get tired," Nan said.

"I am not tired," Laine said. But they both knew she was.

Laine could not keep up with Nan. And Nan started to score a lot of points.

The other Carter girls tried to help guard Nan. But they had their own players to guard.

Hillman went ahead in points.

"You won't be in the game much longer," Nan said.

Laine was very tired.

Coach Yates sent in Val to sub for Laine.

That surprised Laine very much. Laine was the top scorer on the team. A sub had never played for her unless the team was ahead.

Laine went over to Coach Yates.

"Why did you take me out?" Laine asked.

"You are too tired to play any more," Coach Yates said.

Coach Yates did not look pleased. She didn't say any more to Laine. And she did not put Laine back in the game.

Laine had to watch the rest of the game. She didn't get to play. So she did not score any more points.

Carter High lost.

And Laine was not the high scorer for Carter High.

The other girls on the team didn't say anything to Laine.

Laine went over to Tess. She said, "They act like it is my fault we lost."

"Maybe it is," Tess said.

"That is not fair. It is not my fault," Laine said.

Tess said, "You let us down, Laine. You did not do your part. You just want to score the most points. I have told you before. There is more to playing basketball than shooting baskets."

Tess walked away from Laine.

Laine started to get mad. But then she thought about what Tess had said.

Tess was right. She did just want to score the most points. And there was more to playing basketball than shooting baskets.

It was time Laine started to run some. So she would get in shape. And not get tired so quickly.

And she needed to study for the history tests.

Laine called to Tess. She said, "Wait, Tess."

Tess stopped and waited for Laine.

Laine hurried over to Tess.

Laine said, "What are you going to do tomorrow?"

"Run in the morning. And study after lunch. Why?" Tess said.

"OK for me to run with you?" Laine asked.

Tess looked surprised. She said, "Sure. Do you want to meet at the track at 10:00?"

Laine said, "OK. Do you want to eat lunch at my house?"

Tess said, "Sure. But I have to be home by 1:00. Val and Deb are coming over to study."

"OK for me to study with you?" Laine asked.

"Sure," Tess said. She looked even more surprised.

Laine would have a busy weekend. She would do some of the things she should have done before. She would run. And she would study hard for her history test.

But she would still find time to shoot some baskets.